COLOUR LIBELLUS VOLUME THREE WORLD OF THE FAE;

Follow your colorful world of fantasy into the next exciting realm from Anon Di'zain. Colour Libellus Volume Three "World of the Fae".

The realm of the Fae is presented with many of the ancient and hidden world for you to discover and enjoy.

All available volumes of the Colour Libellus can be found on Amazon, Barnes and Noble (Online) and of course you can always make your purchase through Calwelldesign.com or see us at a vending opportunity near to you.

AND AS ALWAYS, THANK YOU.....ENJOY!

Learn more about all the Colour Libellus Volumes along with other wonderful projects that have been created by Melodie Rone and Brent Calhoun by visiting

www.anondizain.com

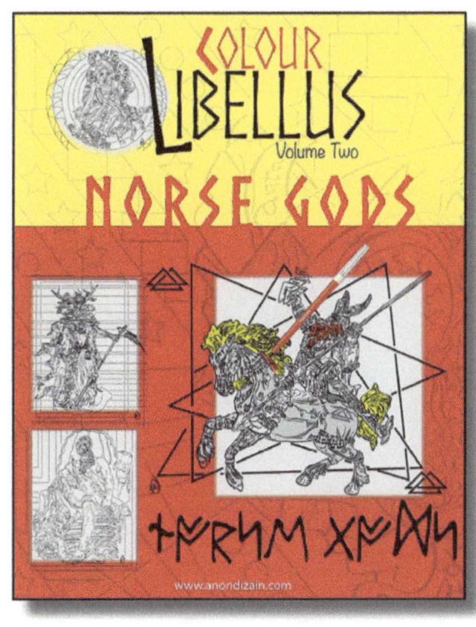